TRADITIONAL STORIES OF THE NORTHEAST NATIONS

BY ANITA YASUDA

CONTENT CONSULTANT
Robin Pease
Artistic Director/Playwright
KULTURE KIDS

Core Library

An Imprint of Abdo Publishing
abdopublishing.com

Cover image: Two Wampanoag men wear traditional clothing during a festival in Rhode Island.

abdopublishing.com

Published by Abdo Publishing, a division of ABDO, PO Box 398166, Minneapolis, Minnesota 55439. Copyright © 2018 by Abdo Consulting Group, Inc. International copyrights reserved in all countries. No part of this book may be reproduced in any form without written permission from the publisher. Core Library™ is a trademark and logo of Abdo Publishing.

Printed in the United States of America, North Mankato, Minnesota
042017
092017

THIS BOOK CONTAINS
RECYCLED MATERIALS

Cover Photo: Marilyn Angel Wynn/NativeStock
Interior Photos: Marilyn Angel Wynn/NativeStock, 1; Matt Champlin/Getty Images, 4–5; iStockphoto, 6, 16; Andre Jenny Stock Connection Worldwide/Newscom, 9; Murphy Shewchuk/iStockphoto, 12–13; Nativestock.com/Marilyn Angel Wynn/Getty Images, 18; Red Line Editorial, 19, 34; Denis Tangney Jr./iStockphoto, 20–21; Ken Canning/iStockphoto, 23; Volkmar K. Wentzel/National Geographic/Getty Images, 26; Jill Brady/Portland Press Herald/Getty Images, 28–29, 45; Jeff Goulden/iStockphoto, 31, 43; John Enger/Minnesota Public Radio/AP Images, 36–37; Arno Burgi/dpa/picture-alliance/Newscom, 39

Editor: Arnold Ringstad
Imprint Designer: Maggie Villaume
Series Design Direction: Ryan Gale

Publisher's Cataloging-in-Publication Data

Names: Yasuda, Anita, author.
Title: Traditional stories of the Northeast nations / by Anita Yasuda.
Description: Minneapolis, MN : Abdo Publishing, 2018. | Series: Native American oral histories | Includes bibliographical references and index.
Identifiers: LCCN 2017930248 | ISBN 9781532111730 (lib. bdg.) | ISBN 9781680789584 (ebook)
Subjects: LCSH: Indians of North America--Juvenile literature. | Indians of North America--Social life and customs--Juvenile literature. | Indian mythology--North America--Juvenile literature. | Indians of North America--Folklore--Juvenile literature.
Classification: DDC 979--dc23
LC record available at http://lccn.loc.gov/2017930248

CONTENTS

CHAPTER
ONE

NORTHEAST ORAL HISTORIES

Long ago, there was a village at the top of a hill in the Northeast region of North America. Under the moon, after the first snow, people gathered in the village's great lodge. As the flames of the campfire danced, the storyteller took his place. He began to weave tales of ghosts, heroes, and magical canoes.

THE NORTHEAST REGION

The Northeast region has a rich landscape. The Atlantic Coast marks its eastern edge.

A building called a longhouse has traditionally been a community gathering place for Northeast Nations.

Marshy lands in Quebec are home to a variety of ecosystems both above and below the water.

From north to south, the towering cliffs of Canada's Maritime Provinces lead to Maine and the lowlands of North Carolina's coast. The area sweeps west to the Great Lakes and Illinois. Thick forests of pine, birch, and sugar maple crisscross the land. There are many meadows, lakes, and rivers. The Saint Lawrence, Mississippi, and Ohio Rivers flow through the area.

In the north are boreal forests filled with evergreen trees. To the south are the Appalachians. This mountain chain stretches for almost 2,000 miles (3,200 km).

Many Native Nations share this vast area. The Omàmiwinini (Algonquin), Wendat (Huron), Ojibwe, Mi'kmaq, and Abenaki are a few of the tribes who live here. The Haudenosaunee (Iroquois), a confederacy of six Native Nations, also live in this region. Their origin stories tell that they have been here forever. Each tribe has different beliefs and ways of life.

The Native Nations know their lands well. They originally settled in areas where they could fish, hunt, or plant crops. Women traditionally gathered berries, wild rice, and maple sap. The forests provided people with raw materials. Groups used bark to build lightweight canoes. The Beothuk of Newfoundland built with birch bark. One of their canoe designs looked like a half-moon. The people put mossy rocks at the bottom of each canoe to keep it balanced on the water.

THE SPOKEN WORD

For most of their history, the people of the Northeast did not have written languages, so they could not write down their stories in words. Symbols and pictures were sometimes used to record things. People also told tales out loud, passing them from one person to another. It was one role of the community's elders to carry on this tradition. Through stories, children learned about their history. They were introduced to important lessons

Children listen to a Native American storyteller at an event in Vermont.

WAMPUM PATTERNS

Wampum are white and purple shell beads that can be woven into patterns. This allows people to record history without written words. The Haudenosaunee wove the beads into pictures. They used wampum to record events and send messages to one another. Wampum are still made and used today in ceremonies and at meetings.

about love or respect. Listeners often had to interpret what they heard to pull out the stories' true meaning.

Many of these tales are still told and enjoyed today. Elders tell stories about heroes and animals playing tricks. Some tales feature characters such as ghosts, giant mosquitoes, and stone giants. Originally, the Native people of the Northeast mainly told their stories in the winter. During this season of harsh weather, people had time to come together as a community. Today, stories are shared all year long. They are an important way for Native peoples to keep their cultures strong.

STRAIGHT TO THE
SOURCE

Abenaki storyteller Joseph Bruchac explains his connection to storytelling:

> *I really became a storyteller because of my own children. . . . I thought that storytelling would be the best way that I could be with them. Because when a child hears a story, I later realized, that story goes into them so deeply it may stay there for their entire life without their really knowing it's there . . . a story is one of the strongest ways to get across that message that they really need to hear. Even though they may not recognize at the moment what the message is. It may come out years later. I think that is the reason I became a storyteller. . . . To pass on to my children and to other children those lessons that you need to help you be a full and complete person in a culture that's constantly taking away those things that make you full and complete.*

> Source: Susan Gardner. "Interview with Joseph Bruchac." *J. Murrey Atkins Library*. UNC Charlotte, October 19, 1995. Web. Accessed January 16, 2016.

What's the Big Idea?
Read the passage carefully. What does this passage tell you about the importance of storytelling to Bruchac? Chose two details he uses to make his point.

CREATING THE WORLD

Animals play an important role in Native cultures of the Northeast. Stories tell of animals with abilities that people do not have. In these tales, a wolf may eat fire. Or a whale may carry a hero across the ocean. Earth-divers are popular animal characters in creation myths. These animals find mud that is used to make land. In one story, Muskrat helps form land. The following is a Haudenosaunee creation story. In the story, Earth is created on the back of the Great Turtle with mud from Muskrat.

The muskrat, which plays a role in some creation stories, is a common animal throughout the United States and Canada.

THE WOMAN WHO FELL FROM THE SKY

Long ago, a great tree grew in the sky world. Flowers and fruit hung from its branches. One night, the Chief of the sky had a dream. "The Great Tree must be dug up," the Chief told his wife, Sky Woman, the next morning. And so it was. The Chief's wife was eager to look into the great hole in the sky. And when she did, she slipped. As she fell, she grabbed at corn and tobacco. She took seeds of beans and squash with her.

Loons, geese, and ducks saw her falling. "We will help," they cried. They joined their wings together and caught Sky Woman. But she was too heavy for them to hold up. The world below was all water. "Let the woman rest on me," said Great Turtle. Once she was safely on the shell of the turtle, the woman asked the water animals to dive for dirt. Many creatures tried, but only Muskrat succeeded. "I will sprinkle this mud over Turtle's back," said Sky Woman.

The land grew and grew. It became the earth. Then, Sky Woman planted the seeds she had carried with her from the sky world. Since that time, the spirits of those plants have provided for the Haudenosaunee.

LAND OF THE HAUDENOSAUNEE

The origin story tells of two worlds. One is in the sky where beings like humans live. Below them is a watery world with birds and other animals. The animals are shown to be caring. The animals work together to create land for Sky Woman to live on.

The images in the story reflect the Haudenosaunee homelands. The people lived in what are now

PERSPECTIVES
CREATING LAND
One Wendat creation tale is similar to the Haudenosaunee story. It has two worlds, the sky and the watery Earth below. A woman in the sky is tossed down to Earth. She is caught by birds and lands on a turtle. Instead of Muskrat, Toad dives down to retrieve dirt. The Wendat call the woman from the sky world Aataentsic, or "ancient one."

Marshy lands in Quebec are home to a variety of ecosystems both above and below the water.

New York, Ontario, and Quebec. Some groups lived in parts of Ohio and Pennsylvania. Marshes, wetlands, and lakes cover this area. Flocks of migrating geese use the lakes. Many other animals, such as muskrats, depend on these environments too.

At present, the Haudenosaunee live all over North America. Some live on reservations in Ontario, Quebec, New York, Wisconsin, and Oklahoma. Others live in farms or cities in other parts of the United States and Canada. The Six Nations reservation near the Grand River in Ontario is the largest Native community in Canada. It has more than 25,000 members.

THE THREE SISTERS

The Haudenosaunee were known as skilled farmers. Their creation story tells of how Sky Woman planted corns, beans, and squash. The Haudenosaunee call these plants the Three Sisters because they grow well together. The cornstalks give the bean vines a place to climb. The squash stops weeds from growing by

THE LONGHOUSE

By 1600, five Iroquoian Nations made an alliance. They were the Mohawk, Oneida, Onondaga, Cayuga, and Seneca. In the early 1700s, the Tuscarora people joined these Nations. Their alliance is called the Six Nations, or the Haudenosaunee Confederacy. In their language, the word *Haudenosaunee* means "people of the longhouse." Once, many families lived within long, barrel-shaped homes. These are called longhouses. The longhouse is an important symbol of community.

A garden in a reconstructed Shawnee village in Ohio features the Three Sisters.

blocking sunlight on the ground. The beans provide essential nutrients to help the other crops grow.

Traditionally, the Haudenosaunee relied on the Three Sisters to keep them healthy. They cooked corn in a pot with beans to make a type of stew. Vegetables were also eaten with game or used in breads or soups.

The Haudenosaunee hold ceremonies to thank the spirits of the plants. The Seed Planting Ceremony is held each spring. During the ceremony, people say prayers to help the seeds grow.

SIX NATIONS
CONFEDERACY

This map shows the traditional locations of the Six Nations Confederacy. What do you notice about the locations of the different Haudenosaunee tribes? Why do you think the six Nations joined together?

Canada

New York

Mohawks

LAKE ONTARIO

Onondagas

Cayugas

Senecas

Oneidas

Tuscaroras

Pennsylvania

CHAPTER
THREE

THE CHANGING SEASONS

The traditional cultures of the Northeast Nations have been tied to the seasons. Groups told stories to explain the changes they saw in their environment. There are tales of heroes who save their people by breaking Old Man Winter's spell. Sometimes, heroes must go on a quest to bring back warm weather.

Native Nations also connected the moon and the stars to the seasons. In this way, the stars became a sky calendar. In many stories,

The changing seasons in the Northeast are visible in the beautiful colors of its forests in autumn.

hunters chase a bear into the sky. The next story is from the Ojibwe. The hero of the story is Fisher. The fisher is a member of the weasel family. It is a small, furry, carnivorous animal. The story shows the Ojibwe understanding of weather and seasons.

PERSPECTIVES
THE SEASONS

The Lenni Lenape tribe call their creator Kishelemukong. According to their stories, Kishelemukong holds a contest each year to split the seasons. Grandfather North and Grandmother South take part in the contest. Each holds a bead, and the other has to guess which hand it is in. When Grandmother is correct, the weather turns warmer and spring and summer come. But when Grandfather is winning, the leaves begin to turn colors and fall and winter come.

FISHER AND THE SKYLAND

Long ago, winter held Earth firmly in her cold grasp. In this cold land lived Fisher, the great hunter. One day he found his son crying. His son asked him to bring the warm weather. "The people of the sky have all the warmth," said Fisher. "But I will try to make your wish come true."

The fisher is native to the far northeastern United States and a wide swath of Canada.

Fisher and his friends, Otter, Lynx, and Wolverine, set off for Skyland. Higher and higher they climbed until the sky seemed very close. Fisher lit tobacco and sent prayers for their success to the Creator. "Now let us try and jump," said Fisher. Otter and Lynx tried, but they fell back down. Then Wolverine leapt so high that he cracked the sky. Fisher used this hole to leap into the Skyland. The beauty of the Skyland impressed Fisher and Wolverine.

Then the two friends made the hole larger to free the warmth. But the sky people saw them and shouted, "Thieves!" Wolverine escaped, but Fisher stayed behind. He did not want the sky people to close the hole, because he wanted the warmth to come down below. They chased after Fisher and killed him with their arrows. The Creator saw everything. He did not let Fisher fall back to Earth but placed him in the stars.

SEASONS OF THE OJIBWE

The Ojibwe remember the story of Fisher through the star pattern that some other cultures call the Big Dipper. The bowl is Fisher's body, and three stars make up his tail. Depending on the season, this star pattern is higher or lower in the northern sky. The pattern shows what season is coming or going.

The Ojibwe were hunters and gatherers. They had to follow the cycle of the seasons. They moved in small bands to share the resources of their lands. A band could be as small as one family or include 50 related people. In the spring, groups moved near maple trees. They tapped the trees for sap and boiled it down to sugar. As the weather warmed up, they moved near lakes. This is when the wild rice began to grow.

By early fall, the wild rice was ready to be gathered. One person steered a canoe, and a second hit the rice into the boat. After the harvest, the rice was dried, roasted, and stored for the long winter months ahead. The Ojibwe still harvest wild rice for food and use it in ceremonies.

EEL RIVER DAM

The Mi'kmaq believe their ancestors have always fished the waters of New Brunswick. On the Eel River, they fished for eels and trout. The people also dug for clams. In 1963, a local town built a dam on the river. It changed their way of life when clam beds became polluted and clams could no longer be eaten. In 2011, the government of Canada began to take the dam down. This is the first part of a project to improve the river's clam and fish habitats for the Mi'kmaq Nation.

Two Ojibwe men harvest wild rice in Wisconsin.

DAILY LIFE

The Fisher was sometimes shown as a great hunter. Today, the Ojibwe who live on reservations hunt, trap, and fish on their lands. These reservations are found in several US states and Canadian provinces. Some groups run fisheries along the Great Lakes. Other tribes have created hiking trails and campgrounds. The businesses provide jobs and opportunities for Native communities.

STRAIGHT TO THE
SOURCE

Obizaan (Lee Staples) is Ojibwe. He talks about the importance of storytelling in his family:

I remember when I was a child, I could hardly wait until the first snow fell because that meant the telling of legends could start. . . . [My mom] would always tell me, "Please try to stay awake because these characters that I'm talking about are powerful Manidoog (spirits)." She said by listening to the legends, you could acquire some power or gift from the spirits she was talking about. So she would get upset with me if I fell asleep. There were a lot of teachings in those legends. . . . A lot of the legends relate to our belief system and our relationship with the animals. And many of those legends dealt with respect. They taught that we should respect the animals and other creatures in this world.

Source: Lee Staples. "Culture and Traditions." *Mille Lacs Band of Ojibwe*. Mille Lacs Band of Ojibwe, 2009. Web. Accessed February 13, 2017.

Point of View
The author says that he "could hardly wait" until stories could be told. What are some of the reasons he and his mom found storytelling important?

HEROES AND TEACHERS

The Wabanaki include the Maliseet, Mi'kmaq, Passamaquoddy, Abenaki, and Penobscot tribes. They live in Maine and the Canadian Maritimes. *Wabanaki* means "people of the dawn land."

The hero is an important character in stories from Northeast Nations. These heroes are often able to create people and change the land. In their role as teachers, they show the people how to live.

A Passamaquoddy teacher demonstrates a traditional dance.

The Wabanaki call their most important hero Gluskap. Stories tell that Gluskap is a god and the first human. In one story he stretches out across Nova Scotia in eastern Canada to sleep. He uses Prince Edward Island, a smaller island several miles away, as his pillow. The following story is from the Mi'kmaq. The story tells how Gluskap fights a giant frog over water.

GLUSKAP AND THE BULLFROG

Long ago, there was a village clinging to a mountainside. The forests were full of animals to hunt. But the river, which should have been teeming with fish, was as dry as ash. The worried villagers sent a man to investigate. After three days of travel, the man discovered the problem. Another village had built a dam across the river. "This will not do," said the man. He went to see the chief of this village.

The man was surprised to discover the chief had yellow eyes. His smile stretched from ear to ear. The chief was a giant bullfrog! The man begged Bullfrog to

Like many traditional stories, the story of Gluskap and the Bullfrog provides an explanation for the way an animal looks.

release the water. "My people are thirsty," he said. But Bullfrog was not moved. "Why should I care?" croaked Bullfrog selfishly. "Go somewhere else."

Then, the people complained to the giant Gluskap. "Do not worry," Gluskap told them. Gluskap traveled to Bullfrog's village. But Bullfrog refused to release the water. Angered, Gluskap grabbed Bullfrog and squeezed him until the river flowed once more. Gluskap promised that no creature would ever again control water. The people were very thankful. Bullfrog's skin has been wrinkly ever since.

SHARING THE EARTH

Gluskap is a hero to the Wabanaki. He used his power to defeat Bullfrog. Gluskap's actions show his concern for the people. The story suggests the value of rivers to the Wabanaki. Rivers provided the people with fish for food. Eels were one important fish.

The Wabanaki made fishhooks, traps, and nets from trees and other plants. To make a net, the people gathered bark from trees such as birch. They peeled off the inner bark in long strips and boiled them. The boiled strips were woven or twisted into nets.

Today, fish and water remain important to the Wabanaki.

The Passamaquoddy in Maine are protecting fish and other wildlife. In 2011, some members began an organization called the Schoodic Riverkeepers. The group is working to restore ecosystems in their homelands.

CANOES

Wabanaki land holds many rivers and lakes. The Wabanaki use these resources for building, transportation, and hunting. Wabanaki builders used cedar and birch to build canoes. They used cedar for the canoe's frame and covered it with sheets of birch bark. Seams were sealed with spruce gum. Canoes made it possible for people to use resources all over their lands.

EEL RIVER DAM

The Mi'kmaq believe their ancestors have always fished the waters of New Brunswick. On the Eel River, they fished for eels and trout. The people also dug for clams. In 1963, a local town built a dam on the river. It changed their way of life when clam beds became polluted and clams could no longer be eaten. In 2011, the government of Canada began to take the dam down. This is the first part of a project to improve the river's clam and fish habitats for the Mi'kmaq Nation.

NORTHEAST
NATIONS

This map shows the locations of Native Nations in the large Northeast region. What do you notice about the different Nations and the geography of their region? How might the lifestyles of people in different parts of the Northeast differ?

Ojibwe

LAKE SUPERIOR

Minnesota

Ojibwe

Wisconsin

LAKE MICHIGAN

Potawatomi

Michigan

Iowa

Illinois

Illinois

Indiana

LAKE HURON

LAKE ERIE

Huron

LAKE ONTARIO

Ohio

Seneca Cayuga Onondaga Oneida

Shawnee

West Virginia

Kentucky

Algonquin

Vermont

Iroquois

Abenaki

Maine

Mohawk

Mohican

New York

Pennsylvania

Delaware

Virginia

Powhatan

Passamaquoddy

Penobscot

Mi'kmaq

New Hampshire

Massachusetts

Wampanoag

Rhode Island

Connecticut

Montauk

New Jersey

Delaware

Maryland

ATLANTIC OCEAN

N W E S

The Wabanaki built several styles of canoes. Each had a different purpose. They used birch canoes on rivers and streams. These canoes were light enough to be carried from one river to the next. They also used dugout canoes on lakes and rivers. The Wabanaki made them by cleaning out a tree trunk. They built oceangoing canoes with raised sides to handle high waves. These canoes were used to hunt mammals such as porpoises.

FURTHER EVIDENCE

Chapter Four covers how the Wabanaki people used resources in their traditional territory. It also covers the role of the hero Gluskap. Watch the video on the website below to learn more about how the Wabanaki link their stories to their homelands. Choose a quote from the video that relates to this chapter. Does this quote support the author's main point? Does it make a new point? Write a few sentences explaining how the quote you found relates to this chapter.

PARTRIDGE ISLAND
abdocorelibrary.com/northeast-nations

CHAPTER
FIVE

STORYTELLING TODAY

Many members of Northeast Nations today are gathering stories from their elders. These stories connect people to their culture. Stories give youth a sense of pride. Young people may learn Native ideas about land, animals, or climate. Stories are also used to teach Native languages to students.

The Mi'kmaq people are preserving their culture through the Mi'kmawey Debert Cultural Centre (MDCC). The MDCC began interviewing elders in the early 2000s. The stories are now available online. The Internet

Anne Dunn is an Ojibwe storyteller living in Minnesota.

makes it easier for people from other cultures to learn about the Mi'kmaq.

RITA JOE

Rita Joe was a Mi'kmaq elder and poet. She was born in 1932. Rita Joe is best known for her poem "I Lost My Talk." The poem is about when the poet lived in a residential school. The US and Canadian governments set up schools to force Native American children away from their own cultures. Children at these government-run schools were not treated well. They could not speak their own languages. As an adult,

Dancers from the Oneida Nation perform in 2014.

Rita Joe encouraged Native youth to speak up. She wanted them to share their stories.

In 2009 Rita Joe died. In 2016 the National Arts Center in Ottawa began a cultural program in her name. It was called the Rita Joe National Song Project. Students from five Native groups created songs based on "I Lost My Talk."

SHARING STORIES

Native tellers in the Northeast share their stories. The Leech Lake Band of Ojibwe run a radio station called the Eagle. One of the station's goals is to strengthen the culture of its people. Storyteller Elaine Fleming hosts a history program on the station. She tells stories about her community that have not yet been written down.

Some storytellers appear at schools and community centers. They also travel to festivals all over North America. The Iroquois Cultural Festival in Cooperstown, New York, is one of the largest gatherings.

PERSPECTIVES

THE POET LAUREATE

Rebecca Lea Thomas is a Mi'kmaq spoken word artist. She believes that poetry can be used to create dialogue. She has been creating poems for more than ten years. Thomas is now the poet laureate of Nova Scotia. She is the first Native person to hold this position. She wants Native people to make their voices heard. She hopes that in her new position she will improve the public understanding of Native experiences.

Mohawk storyteller Kay Olan is a visitor to the festival. She has been telling stories for more than 30 years. Her stories are like those she heard as a child.

The future of storytelling in the Northeast is hopeful. Today, Native artists are gathering stories and sharing their cultures. They are bringing these stories to life in new ways. Film, music, and digital media are creating exciting opportunities for storytellers to be heard.

EXPLORE ONLINE

Chapter Five discusses Native storytellers, poets, and writers from Northeast Nations. It talks about Nations sharing and preserving stories from their elders and inspiring a new generation of storytellers. Go to the website listed below, and watch the video of Mohawk storyteller Kay Olan. What new information did you learn from the video? What information was similar to Chapter Five? What can you learn from this video?

MOUNTAIN LAKE PBS: MOHAWK STORYTELLER FIGHTS STEREOTYPES

abdocorelibrary.com/northeast-nations

STORY
SUMMARIES

The Woman Who Fell from the Sky (Haudenosaunee)

Sky Woman is caught by a flock of birds after she falls through a hole in the sky. She comes to rest on the back of a turtle. Muskrat dives for special mud. The Sky Woman uses it to create land on Turtle's back. This becomes the earth. She sows seeds that become the staple crops of the Haudenosaunee.

Fisher and the Skyland (Ojibwe)

Fisher's son asks him to bring warm weather from Skyland. Fisher agrees and sets off on a quest with his friends. They succeed in getting some of the warm air, but Fisher is unable to escape back to Earth. After he is felled by an arrow, the Creator places Fisher in the stars.

Gluskap and the Bullfrog (Mi'kmaq)

Gluskap arrives to help the village after a giant bullfrog takes the people's water. Gluskap battles Bullfrog until the water is released. After the battle, Gluskap promises the people that no creature will ever again control water.

STOP AND THINK

Tell the Tale

Chapter Five discusses how Native storytellers are using radio, film, and the Internet to tell stories today. Imagine you are adapting one of the stories retold in this book for one of these modern mediums. How would you tell the story in the new medium?

Say What?

Learning about oral traditions in the Northeast can mean learning new vocabulary. Find five words in this book that you've never heard before. Use a dictionary to find out what they mean. Write the meanings in your own words, and use each word in a new sentence.

Why Do I Care?

This book discusses the importance of sharing stories. Elderly people often tell these stories to younger generations. What kinds of stories are told in your community? Have you heard stories from older generations?

Take a Stand

Joseph Bruchac tells that he became a storyteller to build a stronger relationship with his children. He talks about not explaining the meaning of a story. Instead, the listener may come to understand the story's message years later. Do you think storytellers should explain the stories they tell? Or should listeners decide what a story means to them?

GLOSSARY

alliance
a group of people who
work together

ancestors
a person's relatives from
long ago

boreal forests
areas with trees that ring
the northern part of the
Northern Hemisphere

ceremonies
formal events that are
celebrated by many people

cultures
the beliefs and customs of
particular groups of people

ecosystems
particular environments and
the things that live in them

migrate
to move from place to place

poet laureate
a poet appointed by the
government as the official
poet of a region

quest
a search for something that
usually involves a journey

reservations
lands that the US and
Canadian governments
set aside for Native
American use

tribes
groups of Native people
who share common cultures
and languages

LEARN MORE

Books

McCarthy, Pat. *Colonization and Settlement in the New World: 1583–1763*. Minneapolis, MN: Abdo Publishing, 2014.

Mooney, Carla. *Traditional Stories of the Southeast Nations*. Minneapolis, MN: Abdo Publishing, 2018.

Robertson, Robbie, and David Shannon. *Hiawatha and the Peacemaker*. New York: Harry N. Abrams, 2015.

Websites

To learn more about Native American Oral Histories, visit **abdobooklinks.com**. These links are routinely monitored and updated to provide the most current information available.

Visit **abdocorelibrary.com** for free additional tools for teachers and students.

INDEX

About the Author

Anita Yasuda is the author of more than 100 books for children. She enjoys writing biographies, books about science and social studies, and chapter books. Anita lives with her family in Huntington Beach, California, where you can find her on most days walking her dog along the shore.